GRAPHIC

cathy brett

Barrington Stoke

First published in 2013 in Great Britain by
Barrington Stoke Ltd
18 Walker Street, Edinburgh, EH3 7LP

www.barringtonstoke.co.uk

This edition first published 2013

ISBN: 978-1-78112-214-3

Printed in China by Leo

For Doodles and Moo-moo

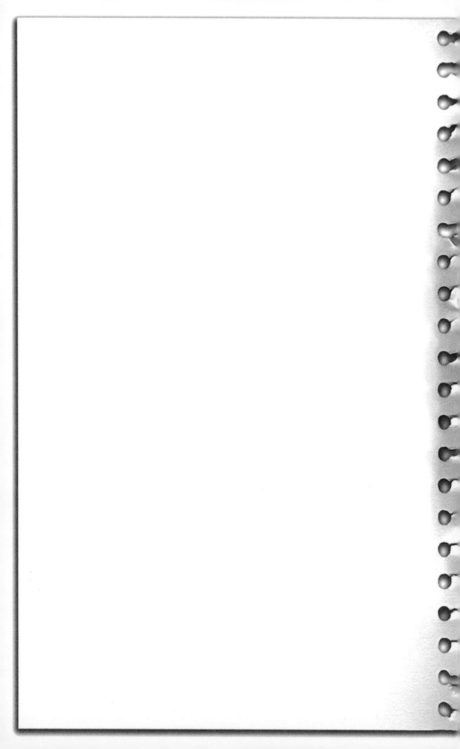

Contents

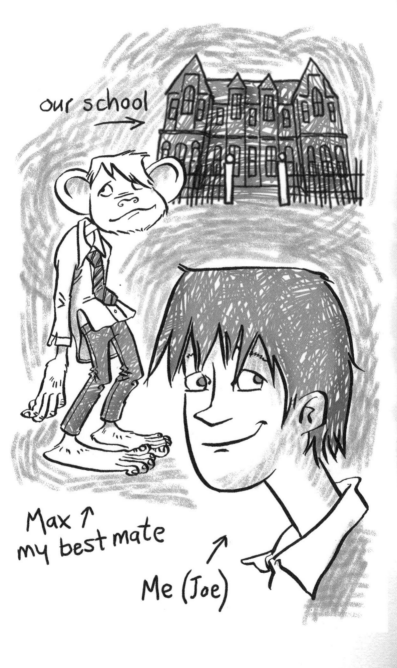

our school →

Max ↑
my best mate

Me (Joe) ↗

Chapter 1

I draw as fast as I can.

I do circles for eyes, two wavy lines for eyebrows and a pointy nose.

My best mate Max is sitting beside me and I feel his arm shake. He's watching me draw instead of doing his work, and he's trying not to laugh. I dash my pen across the paper to make a wide mouth and Max snorts. My hand twitches up and down to add wild hair and this is too much for Max. The desk judders. I look up at him and he's doing that silent laugh thing, when your face goes red and snot comes out of your nose and you jiggle in your seat. It's like he's a bottle of cola with a whole packet of mints stuffed in, ready to explode. Have you ever done that? It's really cool, but kind of messy when it goes off.

I hope Max doesn't explode yet. It would spoil everything. I don't want to get caught before I've finished my portrait of the teacher, so I give Max a look that says, 'Cut it out' and roll my eyes to the front of the classroom. Mr Parks has his head down. He's marking our homework and he hasn't noticed anything wrong. But he will in a minute, because a girl has turned around to see why Max is making a strange noise. A grin breaks across her face and she grabs her friend's arm. Now they are both turning to look back and giggling. I know I don't have much time before Max can't control himself any more, so I scribble a tie with a ketchup stain and a jacket that is too tight to cover a bulging belly. I draw the last few squiggles to show buttons straining over the stomach.

"Joe!" Mr Parks shouts.

It makes me jump and my pen leaps out of my hand. I've been caught. I stop the pen before it rolls off the desk, but I don't look up.

The girls snap around to face the front again. They hunch over their books and I

can see they're still giggling by the way their backs wobble. I look sideways at Max. His face is scrunched up like he's in pain.

Mr Parks gets up from his chair and pulls his jacket over his bulging belly. It's too tight to do up the buttons. "Joe?" he says again. "Are you drawing?"

"No, Sir," I lie. I turn over the page in my folder and pretend to write. I'm not much good at pretending, so Parks isn't fooled.

"Save those cartoons of yours for Art lessons, OK, Joe?" he says.

"Yes, Sir," I say.

"Then you can draw as many freaks and weirdos as you like," Parks tells me.

Max explodes.

"PAAA HA HA HA!" His laugh is so loud they can hear it right across the other side of the school.

I almost gave up drawing last term. I nearly stopped doing cartoons forever. It would be pretty serious for me to give up

Art, because Art is my best subject. In fact, it's the only subject I'm any good at. I love to draw. I draw people, my mates and girls and teachers. And sometimes I draw aliens, zombies, freaks and weirdos. I draw all the time, even when I'm not supposed to. But there are some things I won't draw any more, because of what happened last term. Last term my drawings got me into big trouble. Really big trouble. You might not believe my story, but here's what happened.

Chapter 2

I got told off for drawing all the time last term, in just about every lesson except Art. Obviously it was OK to draw in Art. Double Art on Friday afternoon was my favourite lesson of the week for two reasons. First, because Art's the only subject I'm any good at, like I said. And second, because of Honey.

Before you ask, I don't mean that runny yellow stuff you put on your toast. I mean Honey Jackson, a girl in our year. She's sweet and lush, like her name. She's also totally gorgeous! And she's really amazing at art, which you can't say about the runny stuff you put on your toast.

The best part of the double Art lesson was the end. I'd watch the clock over the door just like all the others in the class. Only I wasn't counting down to the start of the weekend like they were. I was watching the minute hand crawling from 3:10 to 3:15 to 3:30, waiting for the bell. Waiting to be alone with Honey Jackson.

Mrs Hepworth, the Art teacher, would let anyone stay behind in the Art Room for an extra hour if they loved art or wanted to go to Art College. Only two of us ever did. Honey was going to study fashion when she left school, so she would stay late on Friday to use the sewing machine and do work for her fashion folder. I would stay too. I'd sit at the back of the room and pretend to draw skyscrapers or sports cars. I wasn't. I was drawing Honey.

I would draw Honey's long shiny hair tucked behind her ear. I would draw her white teeth as she bit her lip. I would draw her leaning over her paintings. I would draw her cutting fabric or sewing. She was gorgeous whatever she was doing. I was crazy about her. But I knew that my pictures of Honey were as close as I'd ever get to her. She never looked at me up the back of the Art

Room. She never noticed that I was there.
She didn't know I existed.

I didn't mind that she ignored me. Not
really. It was enough just to be in the same
room as her. It was the highlight of my week.
But there was one thing that always spoiled it.
Well, one person. Honey had a boyfriend. His
name was Calum North, or Cal, and I hated
him. He would show up at around 4 p.m. and
come crashing into the Art Room as if he
owned the place.

"Hey babe," he would say to Honey.

Honey would roll her eyes and keep on
sewing or sketching.

"Hey girl," he'd try again. "Let's get out of
this dump."

"I'm not finished," Honey would reply.
"Give me ten minutes."

Cal didn't like waiting. He would slouch
around the Art Room kicking chair legs. He
would pick up pencils or sticks of chalk and
draw rude stuff on other pupils' artwork on
the walls. He would make *ksh ksh ksh* noises

with his tongue and do a sort of hip-thrust dance between the desks. Sometimes Mrs Hepworth would come out of her office and send him away, but most Fridays Cal was free to run riot around the Art Room and do as many annoying things as he could think of, until Honey had had enough.

"OK," she would sigh. "I'm packing up." She'd gather her coloured pencils and slip the cover over the sewing machine. Then she and Cal would leave and I would be left alone with my sketchbook.

One Friday, Cal was even more annoying than usual. He sneered at the Year 7s' artwork on the walls and boasted that he was a better artist than anyone else in the school – which is a big lie. He said his art was awesome because it wasn't on the walls of the Art Room in school. His art was spray-painted over the back of the cinema and the underpass and the shopping centre car park in town. Graffiti was the only true art, he said. His work could be viewed by everyone, every day. It wasn't stuck in a frame and hung in a stupid art gallery. He said art

galleries were for morons with too much money. The best art was the stuff that was free on the streets.

I hated Cal. He was an idiot. He didn't deserve Honey as a girlfriend. No way! He deserved to be squashed flat by a truck on his way home from school. He deserved to choke on a burger and to turn blue and suffocate. He deserved a slow and painful death.

When they'd gone, I drew pictures of Cal in my sketchbook. That was my first mistake.

Chapter 3

Over the next seven days, I drew lots of pictures of Cal. I drew him spraying graffiti on the back wall of the cinema. I drew him being hit by a truck in the underpass.

I drew him being eaten by zombies in the car park at the shopping centre.

Then I drew him being dumped by Honey. I drew Honey waving goodbye to him then making it as a famous fashion designer. I drew her sitting in a limo drinking Champagne. I drew her walking down a catwalk at the end of her own fashion show.

By Friday, I had filled my sketchbook with ways to get rid of Cal and the things Honey would do without him. At 4 p.m. I was finishing a drawing of Honey climbing the steps of her own private jet, when Cal burst in and ruined everything.

"Wapnin?" he shouted, as he stood in the door. He stretched out his arms and strode into the room like he was some kind of celeb. "Yes, it's me," he crowed, and he waved to an imaginary crowd of fans.

Honey ignored him and went on pushing a piece of fabric through the sewing machine. She pressed her foot down on the floor pedal. The machine growled as it dragged the fabric even faster under the juddering needle.

"You not done yet?" Cal asked.

Honey shook her head.

Cal turned to the back of the room. "What's geek-boy doin'?" he asked.

I gulped and felt my face going red. He had never noticed me before and now he was walking over! I stared up at him. I felt like a puppy in the fast lane just before a truck tyre rolls it flat.

"Whoa!" said Cal when he reached my desk. "He's drawing you, Honey. That is so out of order, dude!"

I had forgotten to close my sketchbook. Before I could slam it shut, Cal had leaned over and grabbed it. My book sailed away across the classroom, out of reach.

"Look, look!" Cal shouted at Honey. "He's done all these drawings of you. That's stalking, innit? We should tell a teacher ... or the police! He's, like, a psycho."

I just sat there. I couldn't move. Cal was waggling my book in front of Honey's nose and I could only groan and close my eyes. My face burned with shame. I felt my head would burst into flames any second and crumble into a pile of ash on the Art Room floor. The cleaners would have to sweep it away with the pencil shavings. I'd have to find my way home without a head.

The sewing machine stopped growling and I opened one eye. Honey was looking up at the book. She shrugged and pressed her foot back on the pedal. The machine roared and the fabric whizzed through again.

Cal wasn't pleased. He flung my sketchbook over his shoulder. It opened in mid-air and fluttered for a second then plunged down into one of the Art Room sinks. Then Cal lurched over to the wall and pulled out the plug of Honey's sewing machine. The machine stopped.

"Hey!" said Honey. "Why did you do that?"

She was angry. I allowed myself a small smile. Cal had gone too far this time. Perhaps Honey would dump him. I crossed my fingers.

"You said you'd meet me at the gates," said Cal. He folded his arms.

"I know, but –" Honey began.

Cal broke in. "You promised you'd be done by 4."

Honey looked up at the clock above the door. "It's only three minutes past."

"Yeah, well, my brother's picking us up. He won't take us to the gig if we're not there, at the gate."

"OK." Honey smiled at him. "Sorry."

Something burst in my chest and my heart crumpled like a popped balloon. Honey wasn't going to dump Cal after all. She was going on a date with him instead. She had forgiven him even though he was the most annoying person on the planet. I rested my head in my hands. In seconds, Honey had packed her fabric away, Cal had picked up her bag and they were both out the door.

"Uurgh! I really hate him," I muttered. "I wish he'd ... I wish he'd just go and ... die!"

I leapt up and ran to the sink. I found my sketchbook inside, splayed out like a dead bird. I grabbed it, picked up a black pen from a tray and slashed at the drawings. I stabbed the felt tip into the page until it was blunt. But I was still angry so I began to rip

at the pages. It was harder than I thought. The cover was tough and the paper was quite thick, so the best I could manage was to pull out a few pages. I crumpled some of the drawings and bent the wire rings round the spine. I tried to rip the pages again, but the edge of the paper cut my thumb. Pain shot up my arm and I howled.

"Stupid Cal! Stupid moron Cal!" I shouted and flung the book away from me with as much force as I could. This time it crashed into a jar of brushes beside the sink. It made a terrible noise, like a multi-vehicle pile-up on the motorway.

Mrs Hepworth stuck her head out of her office. "What's going on? Joe? What are you doing out here? Where's Honey?"

I stared at the floor. "Gone," I said.

"Well, I think you'd better go too, don't you?" she said.

"Yeah. Sorry." I picked up my sketchbook and stumbled out the door.

Chapter 4

On Monday morning, the news was all around the school. I was the only one who didn't know about Cal's accident.

"Did you hear?" Max said, when I met him at the side gate.

"Hear what?" I asked.

"About Cal," said Max. He took his phone out of his pocket and tapped the screen. "Here. Look," he said.

He showed me a message. It read, 'OMG! Cal in hospital!! Might be dead!'

My breakfast of crisps and cola flipped over in my gut.

"He's not dead," Max said. "But he's badly hurt. I hear he had a hundred stitches." He scrolled down to another text.

This one read, 'Cal is in A&E! He's a wuss! Needed stitches, saw needle and cried like a little kid. LOL.'

I hid my smile.

By morning break I'd found out more. I'd pieced together the gossip, blog posts, shared videos and texts, and worked out what had happened.

On Saturday night, Cal and his 'artist' mates had been spray-painting their graffiti in the shopping centre.

They were just getting started on a giant skull on the lift doors, when two security guards spotted them. The 'artists' ran. They sprinted down the stairs and out into the High Street. Cal and his mates were fit and fast and they soon lost the guards. But they were pumped up after such a close shave, and so they kept on running. They didn't stop until they reached the station, where they sat on the steps to catch their breath. One of Cal's mates filmed with his phone as Cal climbed onto a wall beside the entrance to do a dance of victory. Cal laughed and punched the air. Then he wobbled, slipped and fell off. When he got up, he found he'd gashed his left arm from hand to elbow. His mates carried him to A&E at the hospital. Cal left a trail of blood all the way through the town centre. There were red dots like coins along the pavement. A girl had taken a picture of the blood trail and shared it.

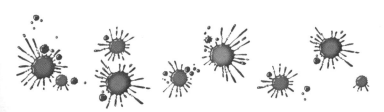

By lunchtime everyone had seen the blood photos and watched the video of Cal's fall over and over again. When he walked through the main gates just before afternoon lessons, they greeted him like a celebrity. A crowd followed him inside to the lobby.

"Is it true you had a hundred stitches?" a Year 9 girl asked.

"Well, no. Fourteen. But they're, like, massive," Cal said. He held the arm with the bandage out in front of him. "And I lost loads of blood."

"Ooohhh!" the crowd sighed.

"Did it hurt?" a tall boy asked.

"Nah! Didn't feel a thing," Cal grinned.

"Will you have a scar?" another asked.

"Dunno. Probably," said Cal.

The bell rang and Cal and his fans began to drift to their lessons. But I couldn't move. I felt sick. Something scary had just popped into my brain. I closed my eyes but the thought wouldn't go away. When I was alone in the empty corridor, I reached into my bag and pulled out my sketchbook. I opened the damaged cover and flicked through the pages. The drawings I'd done of Cal were near the back. My heart pounded in my chest. These were the pages I'd tried to tear up. These were the pictures I'd stabbed with the felt pen. And there, on one of the drawings, was something that made my blood run cold.

There was a deep black slash across the paper. It ran at an angle over one of the sketches, starting at Cal's left hand and ending at his elbow.

I slammed the book shut and put it back in my bag. It was a fluke, I told myself. That's all it was, a freakish fluke.

Chapter 5

I forgot all about the slashed drawing until lunch the next day. I'd managed to avoid Cal all morning, as we didn't have any lessons together on a Tuesday. But the canteen was another matter. Max and I joined the back of the line just as Cal and his mates came through the swing doors. He walked up behind us.

"Hey! It's weirdo stalker-boy," he said. "You'd better keep away from my girlfriend, weirdo-Joe."

I didn't turn around. I kept looking forward and tried to ignore him. I pushed my hands into my pockets and curled my fingers into tight fists.

"You really upset her, you know," said Cal. "She said she'd call the cops if you do any more of those creepy cartoons of her."

"Yeah," his mates mumbled. "Creepy. Call the cops."

I could feel the heat rising up my neck. I was pretty sure Honey hadn't been upset when Cal had shown her the drawings. In fact, I thought I saw her eyebrows arch and her mouth twitch into a smile. But perhaps I was wrong. Perhaps it hadn't been a smile at all.

"You keep away, you hear?" Cal prodded my arm with his finger. "Weirdo."

I turned my head and nodded, but I couldn't look at him. My armpits were sticky with sweat and my collar felt too tight. I knew my face was going red. I wanted to take my clenched fists out of my pockets and punch Cal in the face, but I couldn't. Once again I was frozen to the spot. I wanted to say something really clever to him, but I knew if I opened my mouth only stupid stuff would come out. I'd burp or squeak or barf. I wished he would go away and pick on somebody else. Cal was making me look an idiot in front of my friends, in front of the whole school, in front of Honey.

I was angry. But I wasn't angry with Cal. I was angry with myself for being too much of a coward to stand up to him. It wasn't Cal who'd made me look spineless. I'd done that myself.

The line edged forward. Max and I got our food then spotted two free spaces on a table in the corner. I watched Cal and his mates head over to the back of the room to sit with Honey.

I turned away. I didn't want to think about Honey and what she thought of me. She'd seen the drawings in my sketchbook. She thought I was a weirdo, like Cal said. She thought I was a stalker. She thought I was a loser. I looked down at my plate of chilli. It was already drying out on top of the baked potato. It looked disgusting. I pushed the tray away and got out my sketchbook.

I drew a picture of my water glass. I drew my fork and my plate of chilli. Then I looked up and began to draw the canteen. I drew Mr Parks on the teachers' table and the dinner lady stacking plates on a trolley. I drew empty chairs and the trees outside the windows. Then I couldn't stop myself. I looked over at the back of the room.

It was only a quick look. I just raised my eyes and glanced at the place where I knew Honey was sitting. But it wasn't Honey who met my eyes. It was Cal. I jerked my head away but he'd seen me and I'd seen him. I'd seen his angry eyebrows slam together. I'd seen his mouth open into a snarl and I'd seen his good arm reach out. He had raised his thumb in the air and his fingers had formed the shape of a gun pointed straight at my head.

I stared down at the table. Hot blood pumped in my brain. My mind was spinning. I wanted to hit someone. I wanted to break something. I wanted to shout. I imagined lifting my plate of chilli and hurling it across the room. I imagined throwing my chair and knocking over the table. But I was a coward and I just sat there getting more and more angry. Then I picked up my pen.

I scribbled all over the drawing of the dinner lady and the stacks of plates on the trolley. I slashed my pen across the picture of my glass of water. I stabbed at the paper and covered the pages with jagged, angry lines.

"Hey! Watch it!"

I looked up at the food line just as a Year 7 kid fell over backwards. His mate had pushed him and the kid staggered back. He reached out his hands and found the end of the metal trolley. He grabbed the edge with both hands. But the trolley was on wheels and it began to move.

It was like watching a slow motion replay. The kid and the trolley rolled across the canteen. The kid let go and dived to one side like a goalkeeper. The trolley toppled over and smashed into the counter. Plates and food flew through the air and exploded on the floor. Chilli dripped down the front of the counter like gore in a horror movie. Broken bits of plate skidded under the tables like ice cubes.

The room fell silent.

Then the canteen erupted.

"Woah! Woohoo! Yay!" There were cheers and whoops and then stamping that was so loud it sounded like a thunderstorm.

But I didn't whoop or cheer or stamp my feet. I was frozen with terror. I stared at the plates that I'd drawn in my book, then at the real shattered plates. I couldn't believe it. They looked the same. The scribbled lines on my drawing matched the mess of white china that now lay in a million pieces on the canteen floor.

Chapter 6

After the canteen thing I felt strange for the rest of the day. I was all shivery and I had a knot in my gut. It was still there after school and later that night. It hadn't gone away when I woke up on Wednesday either. It was horrible, a sort of sick feeling like you get before an exam or when you have to go and see the Head Teacher.

Was it the flu?

Was it fear?

Or was it because I'd eaten nothing but crisps and cola all week?

Anyway, the knot got worse after registration on Wednesday morning, when we all trooped into the school hall for assembly. Every Wednesday a different class would take the assembly. Sometimes it was cool, like a funny poem or a song someone had written. Sometimes it was boring, like a History project or messages from a school in another country. But that Wednesday was different.

Mrs Green, the Drama teacher, got up on stage and told everyone to be quiet. Most people kept on talking but I held my breath. The knot in my gut got tighter. I had a feeling something bad was about to happen.

"Today's assembly is special," Mrs Green said. "Today we have a sort of fashion show."

A cold shudder went down my spine.

"You all know that our school play this term is *A Midsummer Night's Dream*," Mrs Green went on.

The pupils nodded and mumbled. Lots of people had a part in the play. Even Max was in it. He didn't have any lines to say – he just had to walk about and swing a lantern. I'm rubbish at acting so I didn't want to be in the play. I'd been asked to draw a picture for the front of the programme though, which was cool. I planned to go and see the play just so I could laugh at Max.

"Most of our costumes have been hired from a place in the city," Mrs Green said. "But some of them have been designed and made by one of our pupils, Honey Jackson."

"Wahoo!" Cal whooped from the back of the hall.

Everybody laughed.

"Yes, thank you, Cal." Mrs Green raised her hand for silence. "We thought Honey's designs were so good they deserved their own show."

My heart began to pound in my chest. This was what Honey had been doing every Friday after school. I couldn't wait to see her designs but I felt scared too and didn't know why.

Mrs Green walked to the side of the stage and pressed some buttons on a console. The main lights went out and a spotlight appeared on the centre of the stage. Music filled the room and the show began.

Honey had got her classmates to model the clothes. As soon as the first person walked into the spotlight, I knew I'd been right. I'd been right to be afraid and to think that something strange was about to happen. Not that the costumes were strange – they were amazing. They were really clever garments, layered and stitched and folded to make unusual shapes. The strange thing was the fabric they were made from. It was covered with a pattern that looked like cobwebs or knotted threads. But it wasn't. It was scribbles.

"She did that pattern last night," a voice behind me said. It was Mrs Hepworth, the Art teacher. "She got the idea at the weekend," Mrs Hepworth went on. "All of a sudden it came into her head and yesterday she bought fabric pens and drew all over the material."

"It looks brilliant," another teacher said.

That was when I knew where I'd seen the pattern before – in my sketchbook! Those scribbles were all over my drawings of Honey Jackson on the catwalk, Honey

Jackson drinking Champagne, Honey Jackson surrounded by her own designer clothes. I'd covered the whole page with angry scribbles!

I stood up, stumbled over legs and feet and bags, and dashed out of the hall. I ran to the nearest toilets, crashed through the door and threw up half-digested crisps and cola into the sink. My bag hit the floor and my sketchbook slid out. I wiped my mouth with the back of my hand and looked down at the book.

Sweat prickled on my skin but I felt as cold as ice. I took a deep breath.

First there was Cal's cut arm. Then there were the broken plates. And now, Honey had covered her costumes with scribbles. It had happened three times. Three times I had drawn stuff in my book and three times it had become real. I leaned on the sink and closed my eyes. The room spun. I stood there for ages while I wondered what to do next. I'd either discovered something really dangerous or something totally brilliant.

Outside in the corridor I could hear people leaving the hall. Then the bell rang for the first lesson. I picked up my bag, pushed the sketchbook back inside and headed towards the Science labs. I had decided to do a test.

Half way down the corridor my phone beeped. It was a text from Max.

'Where did U go? U sick or something?'

I texted back, 'Not sick. Secret project.'

Max replied, 'Is your secret project Honey Jackson? U better take a cold shower, bro. She's way too good for you.'

I pushed my phone to the bottom of my bag. If my test worked then I'd prove Max wrong.

Chapter 7

The first lesson began. While the rest of
the class were doing an experiment with
copper carbonate in test tubes I got out my
sketchbook and a pen. I was going to do my
own experiment.

I'd decided to avoid anything risky for my
test drawing – no accidents or disasters and
no weird things like zombies or aliens. So
I drew a picture of myself holding handfuls
of money. I chuckled. It was a genius idea.
Nobody would get hurt. Nothing would get
broken. The only risk if this drawing came
true was that I would get rich. I made a last
mark with my pencil – a wide smile on my
face. Then I closed the book, put it away and
picked up my test tube. As I held the tube
over the blue flame I dreamed about what I
would buy with all the cash. A new phone, a

computer, an X-Box, trainers and, if there was a lot of money, a motorbike.

But no money appeared. All day I waited. No suitcases of cash fell out of passing cars and dropped at my feet. No winning lottery tickets appeared in my pocket. Nothing happened in D&T or Maths. There were no banknotes hidden in my locker and there was no text from my mum to say that a cheque had arrived from a dead rich relative.

From time to time I checked under chairs and behind doors or looked inside my bag, but there was nothing there. My pockets remained empty apart from a few bits of fluff. All that was in my bag was my books, pens and a pair of muddy sport socks at the bottom. No dosh.

It didn't show up on Thursday either, so I opened my sketchbook again. I turned to the drawing of the money and traced over the lines, pressing my pen hard into the paper.

Still nothing happened. By the end of the day I'd given up. My experiment hadn't worked. I slouched out of the school gate.

"You've got a face like a smacked bum," said Max. "What's up with you?"

"Nothing," I said. There was no way I could tell Max, even though he was my best mate. If I'd said that I thought money would appear by magic because I'd drawn it in my sketchbook, he'd think I was crazy. I probably was crazy.

"There's my bus," Max said. "Cheer up, Bumface. It's Friday tomorrow."

I nodded. "Yeah. See you tomoz," I said.

But even the thought of double Art and being alone with the delicious Honey didn't make me feel any better.

Max ran to catch the bus and I turned to walk home through the shopping centre. I was angry with myself. It had been really dumb to think that my drawing would come true. As I shuffled through the centre, I stared down and kicked bits of litter across the ground. If I hadn't been looking down I wouldn't have seen the purse.

It was under a stone seat outside the supermarket. I leaned over and picked it up. My heart beat faster. The purse was made of green plastic and had a zip along one side. I gave it a squeeze. There were coins inside – I could feel the round edges. And there was something else that felt like folded paper. I looked round to make sure nobody was watching and undid the zip.

I counted £23 and 15p – two £10 notes and a load of coins. It wasn't quite the handfuls of cash I'd put in my drawing but it was money. Not enough for a motorbike, of course, but I could buy the T-shirt I wanted. Or I could get two tickets to a movie instead, with popcorn. I wondered if I should go with Max or if I had the guts to ask Honey. Then I realised something brilliant. All I had to do now was draw a picture of Honey and me at the cinema and I could make it happen.

"Yes!" I did a happy dance around the stone seat.

Chapter 8

I decided to start drawing there and then. I sat on the stone seat and got out my sketchbook. I could draw all the stuff I wanted but couldn't afford. I could draw fast cars and powerboats and maybe a big house for Mum and Dad. I'd get a shiny new bike for my sister and a trampoline and a swimming pool for the garden. I turned to a new blank page. I decided to start with a drawing of our whole family on holiday on some tropical beach. But I stopped before my pen touched the paper.

A kid was crying. It was a horrible noise like a cat being strangled and it was coming from inside the supermarket. It was so loud it was putting me off. I peered through the window. There was a woman at the checkout paying for bags of shopping. She had two kids with her, a baby asleep in a buggy and a little boy hanging on to the handle. It was the boy who was crying. His face was red and puffy

and he had snot dripping from his nose. Then I saw that the woman wasn't paying. She was trying to explain something to the checkout girl while she searched through her jacket pockets. She had a worried look on her face. I knew straight away what was wrong. She'd lost her purse.

I went inside.

"Excuse me," I said to the woman. "Did you lose this?" I held out the green purse.

"I don't believe it!" she cried. "Oh, thank you. Thank you, so much." She smiled and took the purse from my hand. She unzipped it and pulled out the two £10 notes. Then she closed her eyes and hugged the purse to her chest. "What a relief! I thought the kids would have to go without their tea tonight," she said. She opened her eyes and looked at me. "How can I repay you?"

I thought about asking for a T-shirt or cinema tickets. But before I could speak she'd grabbed a bag of crisps from the top of her shopping and handed them to me.

"Here," she said. "Thanks for being so honest."

I nodded. "Ta," I said, even though I didn't think it was much of a reward.

I ate the crisps as I walked home and I laughed. My plan had only half worked. I hadn't found loads of money as I'd hoped, but I did get £20 for about two minutes. But it didn't matter – I would just draw more money next time. I'd draw all the things I wanted to happen too, like me passing my exams, playing the guitar in a famous rock band and being Honey's new boyfriend. Even if they only came half true it would be brilliant.

That night I sat on my bed and filled my sketchbook. I drew motorbikes and jet skis in our garage. I drew my pockets bulging with credit cards and my wardrobe stuffed with gold bars. I drew Cal dead in a coffin and nobody at his funeral. I drew Honey getting into my new sports car and then snogging me on a beach under a palm tree. I fell asleep dreaming about the house we would buy and the jet-set life we'd have together.

I was so excited in Friday's lessons that I couldn't sit still. I felt like a little kid before a birthday party.

"What's up with you, bro?" Max asked. "You got an itch in your pants? You should see a doctor about that." He laughed.

"It's nothing," I said.

Max frowned. He knew I was lying.

"OK," I said. "It's not nothing. It's something. But I can't tell you because it might not work."

"Is it your secret Honey Jackson Project?" Max asked.

"Maybe." I could feel my face getting hot.

"You're going to ask her out, aren't you?" said Max. "Big mistake, bro. If Cal North finds out he'll chop you up into dog food."

I shrugged. Max thought I was crazy. But Max didn't know that Cal North wouldn't be able to chop me into dog food, because Cal North would be dead in a coffin just like in my drawing.

The bell rang and I sprinted down the corridor. I couldn't get to the Art Block fast enough.

Chapter 9

For the first time ever the Art lesson dragged. We were supposed to be working on our clay pots but mine had dried out. I'd forgotten to wrap it in plastic to keep it damp. Mrs Hepworth told me to make the clay wet again, so I put my pot in the sink and turned on the tap.

I looked over at Honey. Her pot was brilliant. It was smooth and brown like tanned skin, like Honey's skin.

"Joe!" cried Mrs Hepworth. "What are you doing?"

I jumped.

"You've ruined it," she said.

I looked down at my own pot in the sink. The water had turned it into a wet lump.

"You'll have to start again," Mrs Hepworth said.

I didn't care that it was ruined. All I had to do was make a drawing of a finished pot and that would fix it. I looked up at the clock above the door. Only ten minutes until the bell. Only ten minutes until Honey would agree to go out with me. But I couldn't wait that long. I picked up the wet lump of clay, put it on a board and headed back to my desk. But I didn't take the direct route. I walked past Honey instead.

My heart hammered in my chest as I reached her desk. I was trying to think of something clever to say about her pot. I leaned over and a glob of wet clay fell from my board.

SPLAT! It landed on the side of her gorgeous pot, like dog poo on a new carpet.

"Hey!" Honey said.

"Oops!" I said. "Sorry." I reached out and tried to rub it off but only made it worse. I smeared the glob of clay and left ugly wet finger marks across the surface of the pot. I backed away. "Sorry," I said again.

I sat in my own seat and rested my head on the desk. I groaned. I'd messed up. Honey would never go out with me now.

At last the lesson ended. The rest of the class rushed for the door. I wondered if I should join them this week and get out of there before I messed up even more. But I had to give it one last try. I had to believe that my drawings would come true.

"Good luck, bro," Max said as he walked out. "You're going to need it."

I stayed in my seat and looked at my ruined pot. My heart pounded again. Out of the corner of my eye I could see Honey at her desk. Then my heart beat even faster as she got up and began to walk over to me. I held my breath.

"Hey, Joe," she said.

I gulped in some air and tried to say something but nothing came out of my mouth.

"Can I see those drawings?"

"What?" I said. I stared at her, confused.

"Those cartoons you did of me," she said. "They're really good."

I nodded. My hands shook as I took the sketchbook out of my bag. I opened the cover and turned the pages. I had to make sure she didn't see the snogging pictures or the ones of Cal's funeral. I found the sketches I'd done of Honey working, with her hair tucked behind her ear and her white teeth biting her lip.

"Cool!" she said. "You're amazing at drawing. Do you think you'll go to Art College when you leave school?"

"Y-yeah," I said. "I hope so."

My insides flipped over with happiness. Honey thought I was cool. She thought I was amazing. She'd seemed to have forgiven me for dripping clay on her pot. It was working. The drawings were going to come true after all.

"Oi! Weirdo-Joe!" Cal yelled. He was at the door. He wasn't dead and he wasn't in a coffin. He was alive and well and he looked angry. "Leave my girl alone or I'll kill you!" he said. He clenched his fists and scowled at me.

I prepared myself for a fight. I knew it would hurt and I knew Cal would turn me into dog food, but it would be for Honey and she was worth it. And I knew I would win in the end because I'd drawn me and Honey together.

Cal had only taken two steps into the room when Honey stopped him. She put her hands on his chest and began to push him back out the door.

"Come on," she said. "Let's get out of here."

Cal looked back at me. "I'll get you later, weirdo," he snarled.

Then they were gone. She'd gone with him.

My brain was spinning. What had happened? It had all been going so well, and then my plan had collapsed, just like my pot. I wanted to hit someone. I wanted to break something. I picked up my sketchbook and tore out the Honey drawings. I screwed them into a ball and threw them across the room. My fingers ripped at the pages, and this time I didn't care about paper cuts. I slammed the book on the table and picked up a pair of scissors. I raised my arms and stabbed the book over and over. The blades sank deep into the white sheets and cut ragged holes. At last I picked up the tattered book and flung it at the wall. It hit a shelf of paint jars. The jars tumbled and smashed. The book broke apart and the pages scattered across the floor. Paint splashed in all directions. Red paint.

SQUEEEAAALLLLL ... CRASH!

There was a terrible sound outside. It was like the soundtrack in an action movie when a car chase ends with a massive pile-up. I froze. Then I heard a scream.

"NOOOOOOOOO!"

It was Honey.

"What have I done?" I mumbled. I looked down at the scattered sketchbook pages. Motorbikes and sports cars were crumpled and ripped. The drawings of Honey and Cal were covered in ugly stab wounds and splashed with the spilled red paint. It looked like blood.

"What have I done?" I repeated. "I drew Cal in a coffin. I drew his funeral. And now I've killed him! I'm a murderer!"

Chapter 10

I ran out and dashed towards the school gates. But what I found surprised me.

Cal was fine. He was standing on the pavement outside. In front of him was a motorbike, on its side in the middle of the road. Across from that was a parked car with a dent in the door the exact size of the motorbike. And beside the car were two bodies. One of them was Honey.

"Oh, no!" I moaned.

Then the body that was Honey moved and spoke. "He's hurt! Call for an ambulance," she yelled.

I blinked. Thank goodness. Honey was OK. She was on her knees in the road beside the motorbike guy, who wasn't moving. He had a deep gash along his shin. There was a lot of blood and it looked bad. I couldn't see his face because he had on a black crash helmet, but I knew who it was. He was a Year 12, called Harry, who rode his motorbike to school every day.

"Don't just stand there," Honey said. "Do something."

Was she talking to me or to Cal? I couldn't tell.

"He nearly hit us," Cal shouted. "He's an idiot. He shouldn't be allowed to ride a bike if he can't handle it."

"Shut up, Cal," Honey snapped. She sounded angry and scared. "It wasn't Harry's fault. It was yours! You're the idiot! You stepped out in front of him and made him swerve."

I knew they were both wrong. It was my fault. I had caused the accident when I'd destroyed my sketchbook. I had to do something to make it right. I got out my phone, tapped three nines and pressed the green button. There was a click and a voice asked me whether I needed fire, police or ambulance.

"Ambulance," I said. "There's been an accident. A motorbike rider. I think he's quite badly hurt." I gave the address of the school and the voice said the ambulance wouldn't be long.

"Help is coming," I said.

Honey nodded but she still seemed worried.

I looked down at Harry. He hadn't moved and a lot of blood was dripping from his wound. He might bleed to death before the ambulance got there. Then I really would be a murderer.

"We shouldn't take his helmet off in case he has a neck injury," I said to Honey. "But we should see if he's breathing."

"He is," said Honey. "His chest is moving."

"OK," I said. "We have to stop the bleeding. Press your hands over that cut and I'll go and get some help." I ran back into the school.

Mr Parks was in the lobby. I told him there had been an accident and that I'd called for an ambulance. Parks said I should go back outside and wait while he got a First Aid kit.

I ran back to the gates and sat down beside Honey.

"Parks is bringing a First Aid kit," I said. "We should lift up Harry's leg and keep pressing the wound."

"OK," Honey said.

I lifted Harry's leg and pushed our school bags under it. Honey was shaking but she kept pressing the wound. She had blood all over her hands.

Harry groaned inside his helmet. He was in pain but at least he wasn't dead.

"It's OK, Harry," said Honey. "Don't move. An ambulance is coming." She flexed her fingers. She'd been pressing the cut for several minutes.

"Your hands must be tired," I said. "Shall I take over?"

"No, it's OK," said Honey. "But you can help. We'll stop the bleeding together."

I leaned over and put my hands onto the wound beside hers. Our fingers touched. Harry's blood soaked into my shirt cuffs.

While we waited for Parks and the ambulance I looked around.

"Where's Cal?" I asked.

"Gone," said Honey. "He's a waste of space. I dumped him."

My heart skipped a beat.

"Really?" I said.

"Yeah. I'd had enough," she said. "He's a bully. He acts like he owns me, and he doesn't. It was his fault Harry crashed and he just stood there, so I told him he was dumped."

"Right," I said.

"But you were amazing," she said. "You knew the right things to do and you were dead calm. Where did you learn all that stuff about neck injuries and lifting up his leg and stopping the blood?"

"Um, telly I suppose," I said. My heart was bursting. I couldn't believe what was happening. I was holding hands with Honey Jackson and she was telling me I was amazing. My drawings were coming true. It wasn't exactly what I had drawn but it was near enough.

Honey looked at me and smiled.

"Do you fancy going to a movie with me tonight?" I asked.

"Yeah. OK," she said.

*

So, now you know why I don't draw coffins or funerals any more, and why I stay away from red paint.

Harry was fine. He was in hospital for a while and off school for weeks. When he came back he took Honey and me out for a pizza to thank us for saving his life.

I'm glad Cal didn't die, because then I'd have to live for the rest of my life thinking I'd done it. I know it's crazy to believe I caused the accident, and I know stuff didn't come true just because I drew it. That's the sort of thing that only happens in books or movies – not real life. But it's better that Cal's not dead. And that he got dumped instead. By my new girlfriend, the sweet and gorgeous Honey Jackson!

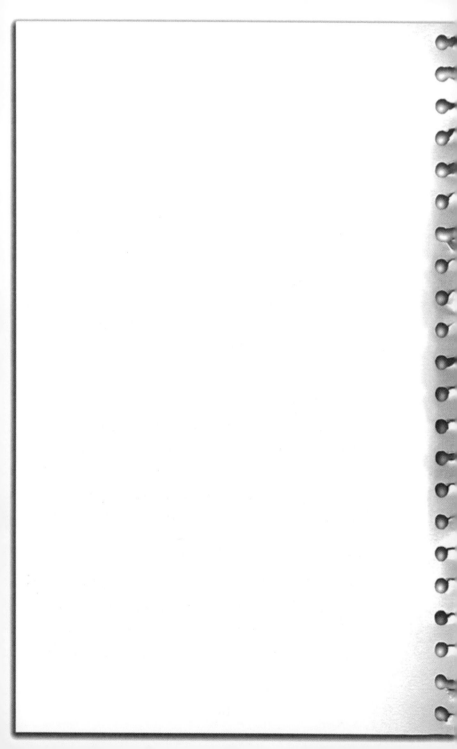

Our books are tested
for children and young people by
children and young people.

Thanks to everyone who consulted on
a manuscript for their time and effort in
helping us to make our books better
for our readers.

More from *Barrington Stoke...*

You Killed Me!
KEITH GRAY

Toby is a murderer. That's what the ghost at the end of the bed tells him.

But Toby's just a boy who loves comics, hates cricket, and gets called a geek by his big brother. He'd never kill anyone...

Or would he?

Gamer
CHRIS BRADFORD

Virtual Kombat is the most realistic video fight game ever. So when Scott is chosen to be a gamer, he jumps at the chance. He must work his way up the ranks to win the ultimate prize. But when his friend Kate goes missing in the battle arena, he starts to wonder if it's more than just a game...

Moose Baby
MEG ROSOFF

They were all waiting to say 'I told you so'. Jess's mum. The midwives. Her boyfriend's mum and dad.

Jess was ready for it all. Bring it on. She just wasn't ready for a moose baby.

Whatever Jess thought she was expecting, she wasn't expecting this.

Pale
CHRIS WOODING

The Lazarus Serum can save your life. Bring you back from the dead. Only thing is, you come back... different.

You're a pale.

An outcast.

It's the last thing Jed wants to happen to him. But then Jed's just been hit by a car...

cathy brett

Cathy Brett lives in Surrey. She's been doodling ever since she could hold a crayon. She decided to write some words to go with her doodles, and the result was her first book for teenagers, *Ember Fury*. This was followed by *Scarlett Dedd*, *Verity Fibbs* and *Everything is Fine (and Other Lies I Tell Myself)*. All Cathy's books have pictures – she can't understand why more teenage (or adult) books haven't.